W9-DES-884

Go fetch, Bouncer!

Written by Richard Powell
Illustrated by Alan Snow

MALLARD
PRESS

One day, a little boy called Bobby was given a very bouncy ball. He took it to the park. His mom and dad, his baby brother Billy, Bouncer the dog, and his friend Rose Marie, went too.

"Go fetch, Bouncer!" Bobby shouted, and threw the very bouncy ball as hard as he could.

What color are Bouncer's spots?

yellow   blue   orange   green

The ball bounced one, two, three times . . . and over the boating pond. Luckily it bounced on Rose Marie's toy boat.

 one duck  two ducks  three ducks

How many ducks can Bouncer see on the pond?

The very bouncy ball flew through the air into Mrs.
Tomkin's shopping basket. It bounced out again.

What is Mrs. Tomkin carrying in her basket?

bread   carrots   eggs

Scratch the cat was lying in the sun. It bounced off her head.

What is the man doing behind Scratch the cat?

eating   jumping   cutting

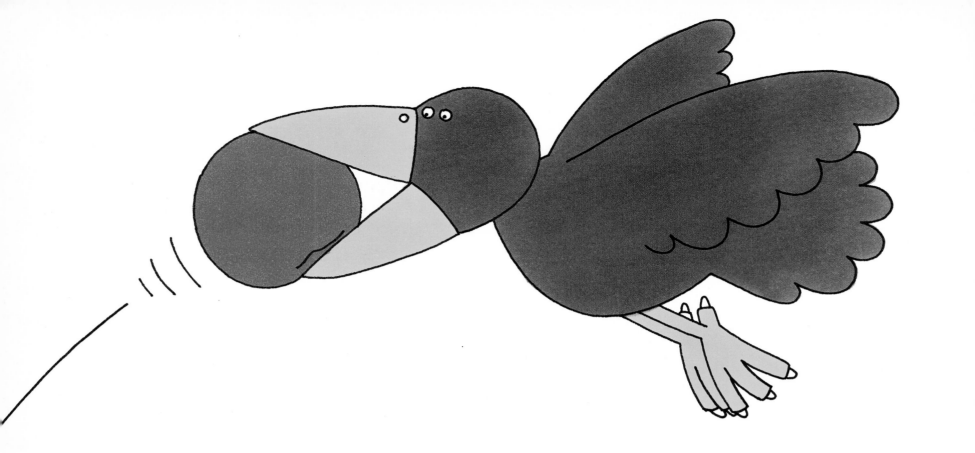

Up and up flew the ball . . . and into the beak of a flying bird. The bird was very surprised. ''Caw!'' said the bird, and dropped the ball.

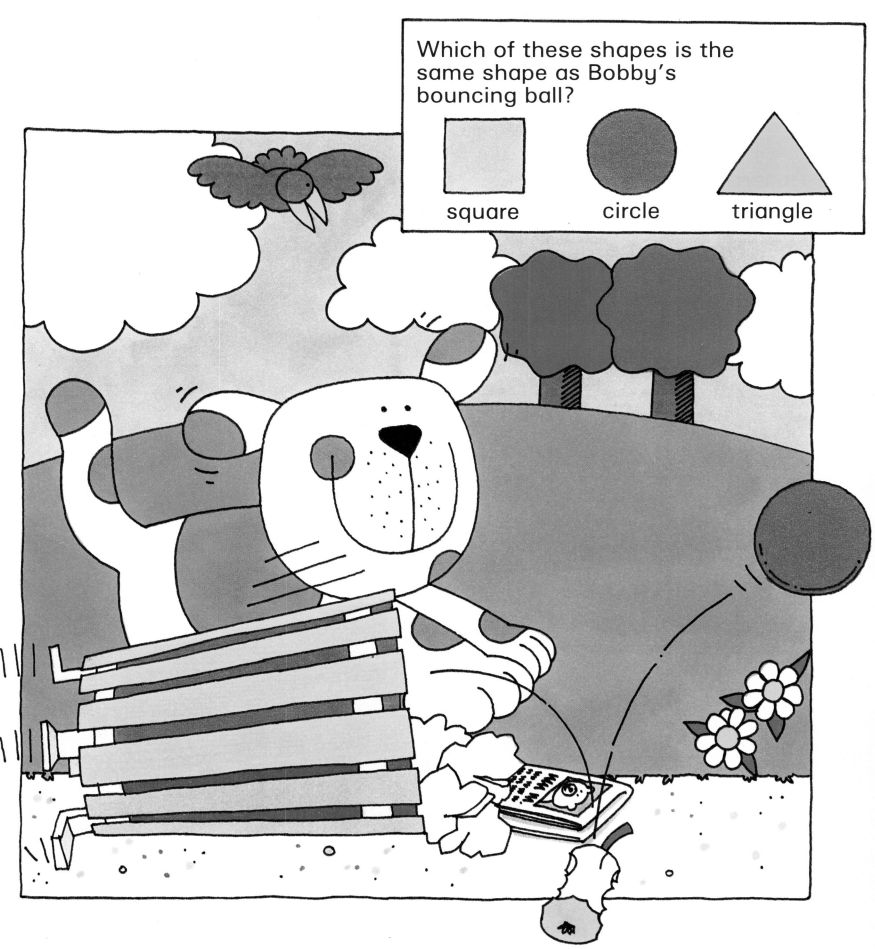

Down and down fell the ball.
It fell into a garbage can. Bouncer jumped in after it.
The garbage can fell over. The ball bounced out.

It bounced into the path of a boy on a skateboard. The boy on the skateboard lost control.

The ball spun onto the path. A man was running along the path. He ran into the ball. Bouncer ran into the man.

The ball bounced onto the counter of the ice cream stand.
Bouncer jumped up, too.

Is the man on the
ice cream stand
angry with Bouncer
or happy with
Bouncer?

The ball rolled into a flowerbed. Bouncer dug the ball out of the flowerbed. It flew into the bandstand. The band was playing.

Where is the ball now?

It went down the trumpet player's trumpet. The trumpet player blew very hard, and blew the ball out again.

Can you see these instruments in the picture?

trombone cymbals drum

It bounced off Bouncer's nose and over a high fence into the tennis court.

What colours are the stripes on the bandstand roof?

red and white 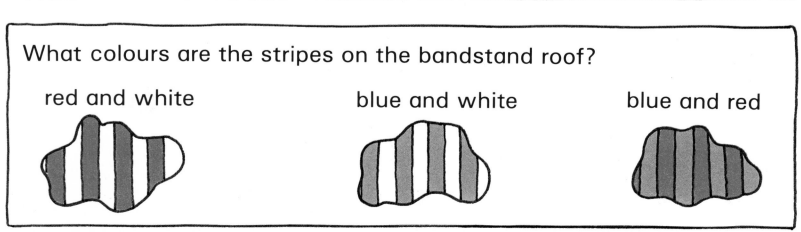 blue and white blue and red

Bouncer was very tired and very hot. He lay down, panting for breath, and closed his eyes.

How many of Bouncer's paws can you see in this picture?

3 three   **2** two   **4** four

Thwack! The ball flew out of the tennis court, bounced on the grass, one, two, three times, and rolled very slowly into Bouncer's open mouth.

What is missing from the playground?

roundabout   swing   see-saw

"Good job, Bouncer!" said Bobby. He picked up the ball, drew back his arm, and shouted, "Go fetch, Bouncer!"